This book belongs to:

To those
who keep trying!

www.plantlovegrow.com

©plantlovegrow 2014
©Elaheh Bos 2014

ISBN: 978-1495457722
ISBN: 1495457729

Special thanks to
Dr. Tamara Soles, Psychologist specializing in early childhood.
For her guidance and for sharing her valuable experience.
www.thesecurechild.com

Thank you to Isabelle Lefebvre
for proving that sometimes angels are disguised as teachers.

Thank you to all the young friends who contributed art to this project.

plant
love
grow

Leo's Words
Disappeared

By
Elaheh Bos

Leo loved to dress up.
He dressed up as a dragon fighter and a clown,
as a knight and a flying monkey.

Leo also loved to dance and play
and sing and climb and hop and jump.

He loved to twirl and leap and whirl and bounce and skip.

Leo loved to make jokes and have fun with riddles.
He also loved to ask questions.
He asked questions about everything.

Then Leo started school.

He was happy to meet new friends.
He was excited to learn new things.

But something strange happened.

When he was at school,
Leo didn't quite feel like himself anymore.
His cheeks were hot and his tummy hurt.
He even felt a little scared.

When the teacher asked his name,
Leo tried to answer
but all his words completely
disappeared.

Leo knew his name.
He knew all the letters in his name.
He even knew how to write it in all the ways:
the right way, the wrong way,
the up way, and the down way.

So Leo took a deep breath and tried again.
He opened his mouth wide but nothing came out.
His words had disappeared.

Leo did everything the other children did that day.
He played. He smiled. He nodded.
He played some more.

But when anyone asked him a question,
Leo's words vanished.
They hid away deep inside him
and they wouldn't come out.

Leo missed his words
and all the crazy sounds
he could make with his mouth.

He wanted to tell Remi
about his wild dragon adventures.
He wanted to tell Emma
how much he liked her toy.

But all day, Leo's words were gone.

When Leo returned home, his words came back.
Leo did a little parade because he was so happy.

The next day Leo went to school again.
He felt like everyone in the whole world
was watching him,
even though everyone in the whole world
couldn't fit in Mrs. Tully's class.
His hands were sweaty. His throat was dry.

He had brought his favorite toy
for show and tell time,
but he didn't have any words
to explain how it worked.
Instead, he showed the class.

Leo was very sad.

He liked going to school
and he had so many questions to ask.
So why were his words disappearing?

Then Leo had an idea.
Sometimes he felt shy.
Maybe his words were shy, too.
Maybe they needed a little help
to come out.

Leo decided to help his words be a little braver.
He practiced breathing in and out.
As he breathed in, he imagined himself calm and open.
As he exhaled, he imagined a strong wind
gently pushing out his words from deep inside his belly.

With his Mom, Leo made a worry box
and filled it with all of his worries.
His mom took the worries and put them away in a safe place.
Now they wouldn't be in the way of his words anymore.

Leo made some worry friends.
He could whisper his worries to his new friends.

Leo drew pictures of his worries.
He drew them going far, far away and getting lost.
That way, they would never come back.

Leo also drew pictures of himself talking to his friends at school.

Leo made up a new game.

He imagined the worst thing that could happen
if his words came back.
He realized that the worst thing wasn't that bad after all.
He knew that he could handle it.

Then he imagined the best thing that could happen.
This was his favourite part.
It made him feel happy and calm.

Since he had better things to do than worry all day,
Leo decided to spend only a little time every day
thinking about his worries.

The rest of his time was for playing,
drawing, laughing, and running.

play time
pla ti
joke time
play time
story time
worry time
play time
play time

And because his words liked to play,
Leo practiced saying his words out loud in front of the mirror.

He practiced his little voice.
He practiced his big voice.
He practiced his whispers too.

One day Emma came to Leo's house to play.
Leo's words were not shy at all here,
where Leo felt safe.

Leo and Emma talked and played.
They had a wonderful day.

The next day Emma told everyone at school
how much fun Leo was at home.
She told everyone that Leo talked at home.

Now more than ever
Leo wanted his words
to be brave at school.

Still, not a whisper or a sound came out.

But Leo didn't stop trying.

Every day
he made an effort to help his words.
He knew they needed a little more practice.
He moved his mouth without making a sound.
He pretended to talk.
He nodded and answered with his hands.
Very quietly when no one could hear,
he made little sounds to himself.

One special day, Leo felt it was time.
He had practiced and practiced. He was ready now.

He took a few deep breaths
because he still felt a little scared.
He remembered the best things that could happen
if his words came back.

Then, Leo whispered to Emma.
Emma smiled and Leo smiled.

The more Leo whispered,
the more his words came back.

He whispered to Remi and Goli.

He whispered to Sophie and Betty.

He whispered to Alec.

He also tried to whisper to Mrs. Tully,
but his words were still a little shy
of his teacher.

Leo kept whispering
until his whispers were no longer whispers.
They became words that everyone could hear.

All of Leo's words were back!

Now everyone knew that Leo had lots of things to say, and lots of questions to ask.

I once saw a raccoon in our backyard. Mom says I shouldn't feed him. I named him Zebra.
I like to eat ice cream. Can you imagine how sad it would be if you were allergic to ice cream?
I like white and blue, and red, and yellow, and green.
Do you have a dog?
I know why you only see the moon at night.
My dog's name is Rex.
Do you know why we only see the moon at night?

Check the free tools on our website:

www.plantlovegrow.com

You'll find free printable pages to make your own worry clock, cool labels for your worry box and much more...

And while you're there, print out some of our other encouragement tools.

Check out Leo's Words Disappeared and came back! The Activity Book.

Good night, Leo. Keep some words for tomorrow!

Good night.

Extras

Make your own worry friends and worry clock by going to the website and printing out the free material.

Worry friend 2 - Zebra

glue

I'LL TAKE YOUR WORRIES FOR YOU

YOU CAN SHARE ANYTHING YOU WANT WITH ME

Encouragement cards

5 4 3 2 1
6
7 8 9 10

You need 1 of these

Cut and assemble

No time to worry clock

play time
play time
joke time
play time
story time
worry time
play time
play time

plant love grow

Look for other fun things to make! We have many free printable pages.

Write your own worry box tag

THIS WORRY BOX BELONGS TO:

plant love grow

Down the ladder we go!

LEVEL 4

SCENARIO: Nothing is working and I feel worse.
I'm not in a place where I feel happy, safe or in control of my emotions.

ACTION STEP: I get away from the person/situation that makes me feel anxious.
I try to go down the ladder again until I can feel better.

LEVEL 3

SCENARIO: I feel like things are too big for me to control.
I don't feel good. Everything inside me hurts.

ACTION STEP: I remind myself that I am trying my best and that I can make myself feel better.
I choose to do or focus my energy on something that makes me feel happy.

LEVEL 2

SCENARIO: I don't want to talk! I feel really angry/upset now.
I feel like nobody listens to me!

ACTION STEP: I think about something that makes me feel safe and happy.
I try to listen to the other person and come up with a good solution.

LEVEL 1

SCENARIO: Something has happened that makes me feel angry/upset/hurt/mad. I want to cry or scream.

ACTION STEP: I take 3 deep breaths.
I close my eyes and count to 10 in my head.
I try to use my words to explain what is bothering me.

plant love grow

www.plantlovegrow.com

Check out our activity book., an excellent companion tool to implement change.

Made in the USA
Las Vegas, NV
13 October 2022